Dear Parents:

Congratulations! Your child is taking the first steps on an exciting journey. The destination? Independent reading!

STEP INTO READING® will help your child get there. The program offers five steps to reading success. Each step includes fun stories and colorful art or photographs. In addition to original fiction and books with favorite characters, there are Step into Reading Non-Fiction Readers, Phonics Readers and Boxed Sets, Sticker Readers, and Comic Readers—a complete literacy program with something to interest every child.

Learning to Read, Step by Step!

Ready to Read Preschool–Kindergarten
• big type and easy words • rhyme and rhythm • picture clues
For children who know the alphabet and are eager to begin reading.

Reading with Help Preschool–Grade 1
• basic vocabulary • short sentences • simple stories
For children who recognize familiar words and sound out new words with help.

Reading on Your Own Grades 1–3
• engaging characters • easy-to-follow plots • popular topics
For children who are ready to read on their own.

Reading Paragraphs Grades 2–3
• challenging vocabulary • short paragraphs • exciting stories
For newly independent readers who read simple sentences with confidence.

Ready for Chapters Grades 2–4
• chapters • longer paragraphs • full-color art
For children who want to take the plunge into chapter books but still like colorful pictures.

STEP INTO READING® is designed to give every child a successful reading experience. The grade levels are only guides; children will progress through the steps at their own speed, developing confidence in their reading.

Remember, a lifetime love of reading starts with a single step!

Visit us on the Web!
StepIntoReading.com
rhcbooks.com

ISBN 978-1-9848-4775-1 (trade) — ISBN 978-0-593-17460-9 (lib. bdg.)

Printed in the United States of America

10 9 8 7 6 5 4 3 2 1

nickelodeon

TOP WING

YOU CAN DO IT!

by Elle Stephens

based on the teleplay "Big Swirl Games"
by Scott Albert

illustrated by Jason Fruchter

Random House 🏠 New York

Brody has cool moves!

He does the Brody hop.

Wow!

His friends cheer.

The friends will have a skateboard contest. Who will win?

They practice.

Penny flips.

Rod races.

Swift does loops!

Brody tries
the Brody hop
on land.
He falls.

Brody tries again.
He can only do
the Brody hop
on water.

The contest begins!

Rod has rad moves.

Swift flips.

Penny rolls.

Rocco zooms.

It is Brody's turn.

He falls again!

Brody's friends
have an idea.
They build him a ramp
over water.

Brody tries again.

He does the Brody hop!

Brody wins!

He did not give up.

His friends

believed in him!

Brody tries again.

He does the Brody hop!

Brody wins!

He did not give up.

His friends

believed in him!